Editor: Ellen Turnbull
Cover: Verena Velten
Interior: Katherine Carlisle
Illustrations: Meghan Irvine
Proofreader: Dianne Greenslade

CopperHouse is an imprint of Wood Lake Publishing, Inc. Wood Lake Publishing acknowledges the financial support of the Government of Canada, through the Book Publishing Industry Development Program (BPIDP) for its publishing activities. Wood Lake Publishing also acknowledges the financial support of the Province of British Columbia through the Book Publishing Tax Credit.

At Wood Lake Publishing, we practise what we publish, being guided by a concern for fairness, justice, and equal opportunity in all of our relationships with employees and customers. Wood Lake Publishing is committed to caring for the environment and all creation. Wood Lake Publishing recycles, reuses, and encourages readers to do the same. Resources are printed on 100% post-consumer recycled paper and more environmentally friendly groundwood papers (newsprint), whenever possible. A percentage of all profit is donated to charitable organizations.

Library and Archives Canada Cataloguing in Publication

Giuliano, David, 1960-
Jeremiah and the letter e / David Giuliano ; illustrated by Meghan Irvine.

ISBN 978-1-77064-442-7

I. Irvine, Meghan II. Title.

PS8613.I845J47 2012 jC813'.6 C2012-902524-0

Published by CopperHouse
An imprint of Wood Lake Publishing Inc.
9590 Jim Bailey Road, Kelowna, BC, Canada, V4V 1R2
www.woodlakebooks.com
250.766.2778

Printing 10 9 8 7 6 5 4 3 2 1
Printed in Canada by Houghton Boston

Jerem
and the
Letter

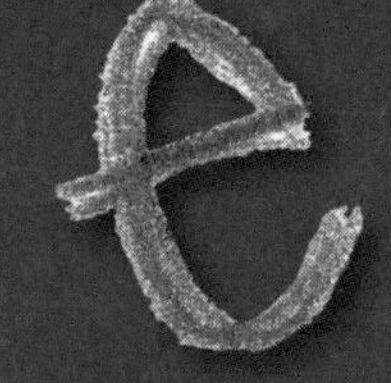

David Giuliano
Illustrated by Meghan Irvine

When Jeremiah went to kindergarten,
he was good at learning new things.

He learned that when the bus driver said,
"Stay back on the curb," she meant stay
back on the curb only *until* the bus stops.

He learned that at school
there are two bathrooms –
one for boys and one for girls.

He learned that when he sees a bear he should drop his pack, back away on an angle, and go to the nearest house.

Jeremiah learned all these things.
It wasn't hard. But what he couldn't and
wouldn't ever learn was the letter ∂.

After supper, Jeremiah would print his name over and over. He groaned, "I can't and won't ever get the letter ∂."

He made the fishhook called J.
He made the little diving board called r.
He made the two mountains called m.

He made the circle and the stick for the a in apple.
He made the stick with a bright idea called i.
He made the little chair called h.
But he couldn't and wouldn't ever get the letter ə.

"Who gave me this crazy name?" he yelled. "It has two e's! Whoever named me should have known I couldn't and wouldn't ever make the letter ɘ!"

He put his head on the table to give his brain a rest. He cried.

His mom and dad tried
to help. That didn't work.

But one day, after trying for a long,
long, long time, Jeremiah shouted,
"I can make the letter e! Look!
It's like a smiley fish looking at a hook!"

Jeremiah made the letter e everywhere.
He made the letter e on his bedroom wall.

He made it on the ceiling. He made it on his dad's forehead while he was sleeping. He told his friend, "That's a letter e."

As he got older, Jeremiah had to learn other new and difficult things.

Jeremiah had to learn how to
skate, which he was sure he
couldn't and wouldn't ever learn.

But he remembered the letter ə.

Jeremiah had to learn how to shoot the ball into the basket, which he was sure he couldn't and wouldn't ever learn.

But he remembered the letter ə.

Jeremiah had to learn how to make up with his friend after a fight,
which he was sure he couldn't and wouldn't ever learn.

But he remembered the letter ə.

When he grew up, Jeremiah had
to learn how to drive a car.

He had to learn how to be a husband.

He had to learn how to be a dad.
All of which he was sure that he
couldn't and wouldn't ever learn.

But he remembered the letter ə.

Every time Jeremiah had to learn something difficult,
a little voice inside him whispered,
"Remember the letter [illegible]."

And he knew that he could
and would learn something new.

Talking with Children about New Challenges

Sooner or later even the most gifted children bump up against things that are difficult for them to learn. How they and those around them respond to that challenge can have long-term implications.

Here are some questions to help you talk with the children in your life about those challenges. This list gives you some questions to start with. Allow the conversation to flow naturally. You don't have to have all the answers! By asking "wonder" questions, you can model that there may be many "right" answers and invite imaginative, playful responses.

Remember to keep the questions open and not to judge or dismiss children's answers. As they respond to the wondering questions, you can just, "Hmmmm," or say, "I wonder about that too," or you can paraphrase what the child says – "It was difficult for you to learn our phone number."

Wonder Questions

I wonder who gave Jeremiah that name?
I wonder why he had to learn about bears?
I wonder what other difficult things Jeremiah had to learn?
I wonder if you have learned some difficult things?
I wonder what helps you when you have to learn difficult things?
I wonder who could help you when you are learning something difficult?
I wonder if you ever hear a little voice whisper inside your body?
I wonder what it says?